AVALANCHE

BRIANNA CERKIEWICZ

MONARCH
JUNGLE®

- Art Seen
- **Avalanche**
- Baby Mama
- Blurred Reality
- Cloud Warrior
- Instafamous
- Lost in Time
- Summer Lake
- The Throwaways

All source images from Shutterstock.com

ISBN-13: 978-1-68021-483-3
eBook: 978-1-63078-837-7

Printed in Guangzhou, China
NOR/1218/CA21801480

23 22 21 20 19   2 3 4 5 6

MONARCH
JUNGLE

Chapter 1

A First for Everything

The bell rang a minute ago. I'm standing on the steps of the school. My body is frozen. It's not because of the cold. Though it is late October, and it would be freezing in Montana. That's where I used to live. No. I'm frozen in fear.

Does anyone like the first day of school? No matter how much you plan, something always goes wrong.

It starts with a forgotten locker combination. This means carrying all your books to each class. But the schedule is messed up. So you're never in the right place. Teachers just keep glaring at you all day.

Then there's the whole social thing. Fitting in and making friends. Wearing the right clothes. It's never fun. But this time it's even worse. This is the first day at a new school. Classes started months ago. That means I'm seriously behind in everything.

The building in front of me is so big. It's scary to think of what's waiting inside. There are 200 kids in tenth grade. My old school had 200 students. I'm talking total.

"You're late."

The voice startles me. A teacher? But it turns out to be two girls. One has on leggings and a tight top. The other is wearing jeans and a hoodie. My sweater dress is not even close to being cool.

"You're late too," I say.

"Yeah," the girl with leggings says. "But on purpose."

"Maybe I'm late on purpose too."

Jeans shakes her head. It seems she's not buying it. "You look like you're about to puke."

She can tell?

"What's your name?" she asks.

"Andrea." I put extra stress on *dray*. It's out of habit. I'm used to correcting teachers. They always read it wrong.

"Dray," Jeans says.

"Really? You too?" I say. "Hi, Dray."

"Uh, no. You're Dray," she informs me. "I'm Cole."

"Oh! Right. Sorry."

Cole just stares.

Rule 1. No full names. It's going to take months to figure this out.

"What's your name?" I ask the other girl.

"Alexandria."

Dray and Dree. That's funny. Hold on. Why is she allowed to use her full name? Is there a test you have to pass?

That's it. Before even trying, I've given up. I'm going home and letting Mom know. We have to move back to Montana. There will be no going to school until then.

"Are you going to the office?" Cole asks. "It's on the way to our first class. You can follow us."

Don't think, I tell myself. *Just do what you're told.*

Chapter 2

No Joke

Where are we going anyway? We've been walking forever. Maybe this is all a big joke. These girls are really leading me to a supply closet. But we do end up at the office.

"Thanks," I say.

Cole sticks out her tongue. Alexandria says nothing. They head for their class.

The woman behind the counter has questions. "Why are you late? What were you doing with those girls?"

What does she mean by *those girls*? "Nothing. I'm new here. This is my first day."

Then she asks to see my schedule.

"You're supposed to be in PE."

This isn't helping.

"Right. Can you tell me where the gym is?"

"All the way across campus. You'd better hurry. You're already late."

"Thanks."

It takes forever to get to the gym. Now I'm super late. The kids have already changed. They're playing basketball.

"Hello?" I call out. Nobody hears me. This is my chance. I'll hide out in the bathroom. Then the teacher looks over at me. It's too late.

"Can I help you?" he asks.

"I'm supposed to be here."

The kids in the room are all wearing black shorts and T-shirts. An image of my gym clothes comes to mind. They're pink. So much for not standing out.

"You must be the new student," the teacher says.

He blows a whistle. The noise comes to a stop. Everyone looks at me.

"You're behind," he adds.

Like I don't know that.

"We already warmed up," he says. "Go get changed. Then give me 25."

"Twenty-five?" I say.

"Dollars," a voice calls out.

It's Cole.

"Yeah," she says. "Mr. Lee is broke. It's embarrassing, really. Asking students to lend him money. Happens all the time."

Who speaks to a teacher like that? It wouldn't happen at my old school.

"Detention, Cole," Mr. Lee says. He doesn't seem mad, just tired. Now he's looking at me. "You still owe me 25."

Alexandria steps up to explain. "Push-ups," she says.

"Really?" I say.

Mr. Lee nods his head. His arms are crossed. This is not a joke. I've never gotten detention in my life. I'm not about to start now. So it's off to the locker room.

When I get back, the kids are playing ball again. Mr. Lee is waiting for me. This is my cue to drop into proper push-up form. I'm on my toes, not my knees. My body is in a straight line.

Twenty-three. Twenty-four. Twenty-five.

Off to one side, I see Alexandria. She's nodding approval.

"You actually did it," she says. "All 25."

"Yeah." It's not a big deal. I was on a ski team. Push-ups were part of practice. We did double that amount. It must not be normal at this school.

Mr. Lee gives a sigh. "Get back to the game, Alexandria."

Yeah, Alexandria. Mind your own business, I think. Who runs this class?

"Grab a basketball," he says to me. "Let's see what you can do."

Chapter 3

No Sweat

Basketball is not my game. I don't score once. Even Cole and Alexandria are good at it. They don't seem to sweat. But they also don't play the whole time. Mr. Lee has to keep yelling at them.

Me? I'm soaked in sweat. My finger jams when I catch a pass wrong. *Ow!* Being the worst player sucks.

The whistle blows. Relief! There's a race to the locker room. I'm thinking about my next class. Where is math from here? This school is a maze.

"Hold up," Mr. Lee calls to me.

Great. He's going to make me late. I'll pretend not to hear him. But something makes me stop and turn around.

"Have you thought about wrestling? I coach the team. We need players."

Is he kidding? Sweating is one thing. But being that

close to someone else's sweat? The thought makes me cringe. There's only one sport for me. That's skiing. "Is there a ski team?"

"No."

He might as well have kicked me. What will I do for fun?

"But there is a ski trip coming up," he adds.

This is good news.

"Stop by the office. They'll give you a form. Your parents have to sign it. Be sure to bring it back tomorrow."

"Thanks!" Mr. Lee is pretty cool. I hurry to the locker room and change.

It's a surprise that I'm not behind in math. But I might as well be. It's my worst subject. The next class is my favorite. Science. At my old school, we were studying plants. Here, they're finishing a unit on energy. Just what I need, more math.

By lunchtime I'm grumpy. Making friends is the last thing on my mind. Most kids go to the cafeteria. That's when I head outside.

It seems strange eating outdoors in October. That wouldn't happen in Montana. It's snowing right now. But this is Seattle. Freezing here is warm. It just rains a lot. Now I notice my shoes and socks. They're soaked through. I'm so ready for this day to end.

After lunch is English. Of course I'm behind. We're talking about books I haven't even read. History is last. Bor-ing.

Finally the bell rings. Cole and Alexandria are nowhere around. They should be headed for the bus. Oh, wait. That's right. They have detention. I've never had friends like that. *Friends* might be a strong word.

"How was it?" Mom asks when I get home.

The look on her face says it all. She has a big smile. Her eyes are open wide. She's hoping it was a good day. That would make her feel better. It's because of her we moved here. She just had to leave Montana. That was after Dad left. Her goal was to get as far away as possible. Now she's feeling guilty. Good. She should.

"Awful," I say. "I'm behind in everything. And I didn't make any friends."

The smile leaves her face.

"But there's this."

She takes the form from me and reads it. "A ski trip? That'll be fun. But it's on Saturday. That's in three days. Not much notice."

"No. But that's okay." It's skiing. What else matters?

Mom signs the form and hands it to me. Wait till my friends hear about it. But we won't be able to talk until later. They have ski practice on Wednesday.

After a couple of hours, I check online. Still, nobody's around. It makes sense. They're tired. Practice is like that. All you want to do after is eat and go to bed.

I lay back and look around the room. Reminders of my old home are everywhere. There are pictures of me and my friends. Many are ski team photos. Awards we've won are displayed on a shelf. Posters cover one wall. One shows the Montana State ski team. The Bobcats are the best. It was my dream to be on the team.

Now that I'm really looking, it hits me. The whole room is blue and gold. These are the school's colors. And the state of Montana's colors. No wonder I'm so homesick.

It's awful being stuck here alone. Seeing my best friend smiling in a photo doesn't help. Does Jamie even miss me? Maybe nobody misses me.

There's only one thing left to do. And that's go to bed.

Chapter 4

Don't Wake Me

A blanket of snow stretches out below me. I tip my skis over the ledge and drop in. Everything disappears. The sky and the trees are gone. There's only white. Gravity takes me. For a few minutes, it's like floating. Then suddenly it all comes to a stop.

"Huh?" What's going on? Where's the mountain? This isn't Montana. And I'm not skiing. Oh, right. We live in Washington now. The thought makes me want to stay in bed.

There's still the ski trip coming up. That's just two days from now. This gets me up and going. But there is one more dilemma. What do I wear? Yesterday's sweater dress was so wrong.

Wearing all black seems boring. But somehow it feels

right. Or maybe *safe* is the word. It's better than standing out. Reminder to self. Buy a new wardrobe of boring clothes.

I also grab shorts and a T-shirt. Whose idea was it to make PE first period? You get all ready just to sweat.

Today I don't feel so lost. And nobody is staring at me. Wearing the right clothes is everything. It's all about blending in. Being early to PE is also a good thing. Mr. Lee doesn't get mad at me. Instead he wants to talk about wrestling.

"Are you sure you don't want to try it?"

How many times is he going to ask? "I'm sure. But here's my permission slip."

The class isn't any better today. Basketball is still not my game. But at least I don't have to do push-ups. Cole and Alexandria do. Well, they're supposed to. Instead they get detention.

These two are always in trouble. Do I really want friends like that? At least they talk to me. It's better than nothing.

Alexandria is standing nearby. "Catch," I call to her.

She turns in time to catch the ball.

"What's the deal with Mr. Lee?" I ask. "You guys give him such a hard time. Why?"

"He's fun to mess with," she says. Then she changes

the subject. "Are you trying out for wrestling? I heard him ask you."

She doesn't wait for me to answer.

"He got me to join, but I had to quit. It's hard to wrestle with a belly ring."

Is that even allowed? Someone could get hurt.

Cole comes up to us. "And I got kicked off."

It sounds like she's proud of this. I'm not even going to ask why. "There's only one sport I like. Skiing."

"Ooh," Cole says. "I can just see it. Spandex from head to toe. A spaceship helmet. Racing down the mountain."

Close. But I'm not owning it. "Jumps and rails are more my thing."

"You going Saturday?" she asks.

"On the ski trip? Yeah. Do you ski?"

"We snowboard," Alexandria says.

"Great," Cole says. "We can all go to the terrain park."

"Sure. Whatever." Inside I'm cheering. *She said we!*

Morning classes go by slowly. None of my homework is done. Last night was spent feeling sorry for myself. My teachers don't care. They just give more work.

At lunch, Cole and Alexandria see me and wave. My plan is to try and act cool. I'll let them come to me. But they end up walking away. What does it take to make a friend around here?

Afternoon classes are a repeat of the morning. And I thought the first day of school was bad. Tomorrow has to be better.

Chapter 5

The New Normal

The next day is not better. There is so much catching up to do. It's hard to know where to start. When I get home, Mom doesn't even ask how it went. It must be the frown on my face.

We're having lasagna. She knows it's my favorite. Really, Mom? This is a bribe. She's trying to make up for us moving here. It will not work.

I'm silent during dinner. After a few bites, I get up to leave.

"You're not done," Mom says. "What's the rush?"

"Homework."

She looks surprised. At our old house, I studied in the kitchen. Not anymore. Now being alone is better.

"Can't it wait?" she asks. "It's the weekend. Tell me about school."

"The ski trip is tomorrow. Remember? I have to get ready."

When I check my laptop, none of my friends are online. That's weird. Maybe Coach added a practice. They must have an event coming up.

Tears fill my eyes. *No! Don't even cry! So you're not on the team. They're still your friends.*

Planning what to wear takes my mind off it. There are two jackets to choose from. One is plaid. It's amazing, in my opinion. The other one is black.

Suddenly I'm too tired to decide. It can wait till morning. It's not like there's a real choice.

Somewhere there's a buzzing sound. Slowly my eyes open. The clock on my nightstand says 5:00 a.m. This must be a dream. Isn't it the weekend? My eyes start to close again. Then it hits me. *Ski trip!*

Everything seemed hopeless last night. This morning I'm excited.

Mom is at my door. She looks sleepy. "Do you want breakfast?"

"I'll eat on the way."

"Okay. See you downstairs."

All that's left to do is get dressed. The black outfit does look good on me. Done.

Mom is waiting in the kitchen. A banana and carton of yogurt are on the counter. "Is this enough for you?"

"Sure. We better go."

The streets are dark and quiet. It feels like it's midnight. We turn into the school parking lot. The bus's bright headlights are shining. Even as cars drop kids off, it's oddly quiet. They all must be half asleep.

Mom starts to get out of the car with me. "Can I help you with your skis?"

"No thanks. I've got it."

A pile of gear is on the ground. It's mostly snowboards. *Sigh.* Another reminder of being different. The driver who is loading gear takes my skis.

Mom waves. Without thinking, I say goodbye. *Shoot! It's too late to take it back.* Now she thinks I'm not mad anymore.

Cole and Alexandria look up when I get on the bus. Of course they didn't save me a seat. The one I end up with is next to an adult. My plan is to sleep if she talks to me.

Mr. Lee is seated in the front. He looks back at us, then says something to the driver. The door is about to close. That's when a guy runs onto the bus.

There's only one seat left. It's across from mine. He's coming down the aisle. Our eyes meet. Then he gives a little grin. Oh, wow! This guy is cute. Wait. His eyes are looking past me. It's someone behind me. Ugh, a girl. And she's smiling back. *Sigh.*

As the bus leaves the lot, my eyes close. It's a two-hour drive. In Montana, the ski resort was minutes from our house. *Might as well relax.*

My thoughts drift to the cute guy. What's his name, I wonder. Maybe that girl is just his friend. I'll have to look for him later.

The woman next to me is speaking. That's when I close my eyes to sleep.

The next thing I know, there's a nudge in my side. "Huh?"

"Time to wake up," the woman says. "We're here."

Mr. Lee stands and gives instructions. We're to get off the bus a row at a time. I'm one of the first out. Alexandria and Cole are near the back. This gives me time to get my gear. I want to be ready when they get off.

Maybe Cole wasn't serious about skiing together. That will be embarrassing.

Chapter 6

On Edge

"You look great," Cole says. "Love your outfit. It's really cute."

If she only knew. Thank goodness I didn't go with the plaid.

Alexandria looks half awake. She grunts something. It sounds like hello.

"Let's go," Cole says. "We're wasting time."

We're in line for the chairlift. It's really happening. *Don't look too excited,* I tell myself. Seeing the groomed snow brings me down a little. Powder is much better.

As the chair scoops us up, Cole nudges me. "Watch this guy," she says.

It's a skier below us. A patch of moguls are in his path. He's going too fast and crashes. Cole laughs. "What a bomber," she says.

This makes me feel a little nervous. That could happen to me. Then I'll blow my chance with Cole.

We get off the lift. "Lead the way," Cole says to me.

It's too late to turn back now. "Sure."

Normally I'd do a warm-up run. But that won't impress her. I push off hard and head downhill. For the first jump, I pop the takeoff, then move into a tail grab. It's a classic pose. Skis cross to one side behind you. One hand grabs the opposite ski. What an easy move. But it doesn't look it.

The next jump shoots me high into the air. My arms spin, taking me in a full circle. I skip the third jump and head for the rails. Rails are steel bars fixed into the ground. They can be tricky. Falling on one is the worst. It happened to me only once. But the bruise lasted forever.

Falling is not an option. So the flat bar is where I start. With good speed going in, I jump up and slide sideways. The next bar is round. I spin off and land backward. Can Cole do that?

I spin some circles, called 360s. And now for the last rail. This one is shaped like a rainbow. Speed is everything. Too little? You won't make it over the top. Too much and you shoot off and land flat. I keep my balance and ride it to the end.

Looking back, I spot Cole and Alexandria. It's too far to see their faces. There's no telling if they're impressed.

Alexandria goes next. She does grabs on the jumps but no spins. And she skips the rails.

"You're good," she calls to me.

"Yeah, well. I've been doing it for a while. Since I was two years old."

Now it's Cole's turn. She copies all my moves. That's until she gets to the second rail. Skiing backward for a snowboarder is different. I'm curious.

She's got good speed coming in. At the end of the rail, she turns and twists her body. She does a 180 off. Her opposite foot is in front. Nice.

After a couple of spins, she heads for the rainbow. Huh? She's coming back. Why the change of mind? Now she's headed right toward me. *Is she going to stop?* At the last second she slashes. Her board kicks up a spray of snow.

"Hey," she says.

"Hey," I say back.

"What do you think?"

That you missed the last rail. But I'd never say it to her face. "That was fun."

"What else can you do?" she asks.

Like what I did wasn't enough?

Chapter 7

Downhill from Here

Cole goes back to the rainbow rail. When she gets it, I'll do some fancier tricks. There's no need to show off. For now, I pretend not to watch. Why do I even care? Maybe because that's what real friends do.

Some of the kids from our school are nearby. One is the guy from the bus. He's the one who I wished smiled at me. There's no sign of any girlfriend.

Just as he looks over, Cole calls out.

"Woo!"

She's on the rail! *Come on, make it.* But she slides off. On the next try, she bails. *Ouch!* Right on her face. When she stands up, I see blood. It's coming from her nose.

I ball up some snow. "Here. Catch."

She presses the ball to her nose. It starts to look like a cherry snow cone. "Gross," she says, staring at it.

There's this look on her face. It's like the wheels in her brain are turning. At the same time, a skier passes by. No way! She wouldn't really do it.

Whomp! Her aim is perfect. The ball hits him square in the back. He flashes his middle finger. Cole just laughs.

"Was that Mr. Lee?" Alexandria asks. "We'd better go."

"Why?" I say. "There's a lot more to do."

Cole is walking away. "The best snow is over here."

"Over where?" I ask. There is nothing but trees around.

"There's a lift. Come on."

It's happening again. I'm following Cole to who knows where. But she's right. We do come to a chairlift. A map is posted. It shows a few runs. They line the edge of the ski area. Most have moguls. Snowboarders I know don't like moguls. It makes me wonder what she's up to.

"Come on, Dray!" Cole says. She and Alexandria are in line for the lift.

"Coming!"

"So," Cole says once we're seated. "What do you think of Mr. Lee?"

"He's okay." I'm careful not to say too much. Saying the wrong thing could cost me. So I change the subject. "Are there any guys you like?"

Alexandria shrugs. Cole is silent.

Wrong again. I'll never figure this out. "Which run are we going to take?"

"I'll show you," Cole says. "Let's get to the top first."

I'm quiet the rest of the ride. The sun feels good on my face. It's a perfect day for skiing.

Chapter 8

Powder Fever

Cole leads us to the boundary line. A sign is posted on the fence. A word is printed in big red letters. *DANGER!*

"Let's go in here," she says.

"But the sign," Alexandria says. "This is an avalanche zone."

"They just don't want to get sued," Cole says.

Alexandria looks at me. "What do you think?"

She's asking the wrong person. Skiing out-of-bounds would always be my first choice. That's where the best snow is. But you also have to use your head.

None of us knows this mountain. It's hard to tell how loose the snow is. There's something else that worries me a little. It's gotten windy.

We don't have the right gear for an avalanche. You

at least need a beacon and a shovel. Worst of all, nobody knows where we are. It's probably not a good idea.

To Cole this is a test. She doesn't think I'll do it. But she also doesn't know me. Right now my mind is on the powder. "Sure," I say. "Let's go."

Cole looks around. Then she climbs over the fence. We follow.

Seeing a track makes me feel better. Other people have skied here. Not today, though. There's a layer of fresh snow.

We follow the track to a bowl-shaped slope. The surface is smooth. We're getting the first tracks of the day. This is perfect. Cole motions at me to go.

As I drop in, snow comes up to my knees. I bounce up and do zigzags. It's a fun, safe move. This gives me a feel for the weight of the snow. Now my skis are pushing through the powder. Wide turns make it feel like surfing. Then the skis take over. They move beneath me. I'm going double the speed. It's like floating. There is no better feeling.

About halfway down, I stop to look back. My tracks are smoothly linked *S*-shapes.

Cole is coming down the hill. Her tracks look like *C*s. She's moving slowly. Her rhythm seems off. Has she snowboarded in powder before?

Alexandria is still near the top of the mountain. It

seems like she's got too much speed. Then, going into a turn, her arms start swinging. I'm not a snowboarder, but I know good form. This is not it. If her weight doesn't shift, she'll fall. I can't bear to watch.

Cole stops beside me. It's the first time she hasn't looked mad or bored.

"Is Alexandria coming?" I ask.

"Yeah, here she comes now."

"How long has she been doing this?"

"About a year," Cole says. "I've been doing it since I was six."

"Really?"

Alexandria finally joins us. "I'm exhausted," she says.

My eyes scan the hill below. There should be a chairlift somewhere around here. If not, we'll have to hike. But not one lift is in sight. The one we took to get here is behind a ridge. We'll just have to head in that direction.

"This whole day has been great," Cole says. "No school. No Mr. Lee. Can you hear me, Lee?" she yells.

"Shhh," Alexandria says. "You'll set off an avalanche."

"That's a myth," Cole says. "Noise doesn't cause them."

Then the mountain echoes back. "Lee, Lee, Lee."

The three of us freeze.

Chapter 9

Blindsided

Whumpf!

A deep rumbling noise surrounds us. Didn't anyone check the forecast? No. This is my fault. The signs were there. It had gotten a lot warmer since this morning. And the wind had picked up. All that new snow was a sign too. It wasn't stable. I never should have agreed to ski here. Trying to impress Cole was not worth it.

The only shelter around is a large rock. Quickly I pop off my skis. "Move!"

Cole is coming. She left her snowboard behind. Alexandria is stuck. She's fully attached to her board. Cole and I run back to help her. We get one foot free. The other binding won't release.

"We have to hurry!" I yell. "Can you push off and slide?"

A huge white cloud is coming down the mountain. It's covering everything in its path.

"Let's each grab an arm!" I tell Cole. "We'll pull her."

We make it to the rock. "Get as close as you can. And hold hands," I say. "We need to stay together."

Then the snow hits. Everything is white. We're inside a huge cloud of powder. Someone is jerking my arm. It's the one holding Alexandria. Then something heavy hits my back. I'm being lifted and pulled away. All the flipping makes it hard to tell up from down. Finally the bouncing slows. The snow around me is heavy.

My mind is racing. *Calm down and think!* The snow will be like concrete once it settles. Before then, I need to make an air pocket.

Someone squeezes my hand. Is it Cole? Alexandria? At one point I'd been holding on to both girls. Only a glove is in my other hand.

It takes a few seconds to clear snow from my face. There should be enough air for 30 minutes. Hopefully we won't be here that long.

Now whoever is beside me needs air. I feel around for a head and clear the snow away. "Take a deep breath," I say.

There's a faint, "I'm okay." It's Cole.

So the glove belongs to Alexandria. I'm able to slip it

into my pocket. She'll need it when we find her. The first job is to get out of here.

There are two options. We can dig out or wait for help. Both have their problems. If I start digging, we could lose our air. Waiting means we could die. Nobody knows to look for us here.

We can't risk it. I'll have to dig us out. But which way is up? There's a trick to this that Coach taught us. You spit and then dig in the opposite direction.

After a few swim-like strokes, I break out. My goggles are foggy. I push them up. It's so good to see sky.

Next I get Cole out. She gasps when she gets to the surface. Her goggles hang around her neck.

"Are you okay?" I ask her.

"I think so. Where's Alexandria?"

My head is spinning. It's like being back in the avalanche.

Cole just stares at me. "She's gone?"

"We'll find her. She can't be far."

"Ah yeah, she can."

The pressure is getting to me. Cole can't know that I'm scared.

Chapter 10

Backtracking

The mountain looks totally different. Above us is a rocky slope. There is no snow. There are no trees. Below us is a valley of white. But there is something. Half a snowboard is sticking out of the snow.

"Listen, Cole. We need help. Do you have a phone?"

She looks at me like I'm from Mars. "Duh. You don't?"

"Just call for help," I tell her. There isn't time for attitude.

Cole digs her phone out of her pocket. Nothing happens when she pushes the button.

"The battery might be cold," I say. "Try breathing on it."

After a few breaths, she tries the phone again. It still doesn't turn on.

"Okay," I say. "New plan. We'll find Alexandria ourselves. Do you know when you lost her?"

"Pretty much right away."

That means one thing. Alexandria could be anywhere.

"Let's go back to the rock," I say.

"You mean the one we hid behind?" Cole looks around and then back at me. "How will we find it?"

She's right. Snow stretches out in every direction. I drop Alexandria's glove to mark our spot.

"We have to try," I say. "It's our only chance of finding her. We'll go in two different directions."

As we head uphill, she calls out.

"Dray!"

"Did you find the rock?"

"No, I found *her*! Hurry." Cole is waving me over.

"Okay. Here I am. Where is she?"

"There! See the arm."

Something is wrong with this picture. The sleeve is blue. Alexandria's jacket is black. And the hand is frozen solid. It looks like a claw.

"Cole, I don't think—"

Suddenly she screams and backs away. This is definitely not Alexandria. It's a man. His eyelashes and beard sparkle with snow. His skin is gray. There's no doubt that he's dead.

For a quick second, I think I might cry. But then Cole

will too. Nothing can be done for this guy. Alexandria still has a chance. We have to find her.

Cole is sitting on the ground. Her knees are pulled to her chest. She's shaking. Is it fear? Or is it because of the cold?

"Hey, it's okay." I reach down and touch her shoulder. She pulls away. "Cole! We need to find Alexandria."

This girl is not going to be much help. I'll have to find Alexandria myself. If she's buried somewhere, every second counts.

Chapter 11

She's Alive!

It doesn't take long to find the rock. And Alexandria's other glove is close by. Now I just need to find her.

Every few feet, I stop and dig a hole. So far I've only found a ski pole. But it quickly becomes a useful tool. Poking into the snow is much faster than digging. Once in a while, I look back at Cole. The dead man's arm is also in sight. It almost looks like he's waving.

I'm running out of spots to look. Then something catches my eye. It's part of a snowboard. "Alexandria?" I call.

Sounds are coming from below. Not words but still something. I drop to my knees and start digging. "Cole! Come here!"

First an arm appears. The sleeve of the jacket is black.

And there is no glove on the hand. My heart is beating fast. "This could be her! For real this time!"

The hand waves. It *is* Alexandria! She's alive! I hope she's not panicking like Cole. It will be hard managing for all three of us.

Part of a face appears as I dig deeper. "Alexandria!"

"Dray."

"Yes! Can you breathe? Here. Let me brush this snow away."

A bit of snow goes into her mouth. She sputters as my hand moves across her face. Then her arms are around my neck.

"Okay, okay," I say with a smile. "You'll have to let go if you want out."

"Right!" Her grip relaxes. "I'm so glad to see you."

"Are you hurt? Is anything broken? Can you tell?" There's a look of pain on her face.

"My leg really hurts. My foot's caught in the snowboard."

"I'm going to get you out."

"Where's Cole?" she asks. "Is she okay?"

"Yes, she's fine. Just in shock. Cole!" I shout. "I've found Alexandria! Come help me."

After a moment, Cole appears. Her eyes are red from crying. Snow is stuck to her face. The white eyelashes and eyebrows look so funny. It's hard not to laugh. Too bad I don't have my phone. This would make a great picture.

She drops down beside Alexandria and hugs her.

"What happened to you?" Alexandria asks.

"She's been so worried about you," I say.

Cole glances at me. I give her a look. It says, "Don't say anything about the dead guy." She doesn't. All I need now is for Alexandria to freak out.

"She's stuck," I explain. "We have to dig her out."

Cole nods. She starts scooping out handfuls of snow.

Chapter 12

Okay, Not Okay

Alexandria's hand looks frozen. Her glove! I go grab it and come back. Cole is still digging. Most of Alexandria's upper body is showing.

"Good job," I say. A look of satisfaction is on her face. That's twice in one day she doesn't look mad or bored. It must be a record. "Pull out her phone."

Cole holds it up. "Already did." But then she turns it on. The phone is dead.

Alexandria looks like she's about to cry.

"It's okay," I say. "We're going to get you out." But it's not okay until we're all safe. "We need to do one thing at a time. Come on, Cole. Let's finish getting Alexandria out."

After some digging, we see knees. "Can you move your leg?" I ask her.

She tries to move and gives a gasp. "It hurts too much."

The digging continues. Cole tries to free Alexandria's good leg. I'm working on the one that's hurt. It's clear to me now. My idea of hiking back won't work. Alexandria can't walk.

Finally I get down to her boot. Her foot is turned at an odd angle. She may have a broken leg. Cole cannot see this. What job can I give her to do?

"Go find my other pole. Please? It's over there somewhere." I'm pointing away from the dead body. "We can use it as a crutch."

She nods and heads off. It doesn't matter if the pole is found. Just as long as she's gone.

"Okay, Alexandria. Let's get this binding off." Now I'm holding her under the armpits. "I'm going to try to lift you."

Having some help would make this easier. But the image of a freaked-out Cole comes to mind. That would leave me with two helpless people.

Slowly, I pull Alexandria out. It's hard not to bump her leg. A look of pain is on her face.

"I don't think I can walk. Not even with crutches."

"It's okay. Here comes Cole. She doesn't have the pole anyway."

From far away, she looks okay. But goggles are

hiding her eyes. Please. No more drama. As she gets closer, the goggles come off. She's not looking at us. It could be shock.

"Couldn't find it," she mumbles to me.

"It's okay."

None of us speaks. The only sound is the wind blowing snow around.

Chapter 13

Not Cool, Cole

My watch says it's almost noon. At four we're supposed to be on the bus. Until then, nobody will know we're missing. Finding us will take a long time. This is the last place anyone will look.

Both Cole and I can walk. One of us has to go get help. A plan plays out in my head. Cole knows the mountain best. She can snowboard down. I'd be walking in ski boots. That would take too long. It makes more sense for her to go.

But she might panic again and get lost. That's the last thing we need. Then we may never get rescued. What if she stayed? Something could still go wrong. Another avalanche might hit. But at least she'd be with Alexandria. Why do I care? I'll be dead if that happens.

Neither plan is good. But I can't be in two places at once. "I'm going to get help."

Alexandria nods.

Cole reaches out to grab my jacket. "You're just going to leave us?"

"We can't wait. It could be hours until we're found. Alexandria needs a doctor."

"Can't I go?" Cole asks. She's looking over at the dead body. My original idea was right. She'll totally panic if she goes.

"No, it's got to be me. Because …" What can I make up that she'll buy? "Because I know how to find my way. I use the sun and shadows."

Cole blinks at me. "You do?"

Of course not. But this is too good to pass up. "Yeah, my mom taught me. She's an astronaut." Mom works at a bank. She'd laugh if she heard this. Suddenly I miss her. I'm glad I said goodbye before the trip. Even though it was by mistake.

"Okay," Cole says. She sits down next to Alexandria.

I wander away to think. *Where is that chairlift?* It's hard to know. Any path is gone. The mountain is all rocks and branches.

A tug at my arm makes me jump. The dead man has come back to life! My heart is beating fast. But it's just

Cole. Must be all those shows about zombies I watch. "What are you doing?" I ask her.

"Don't leave us alone with him," Cole says. "And Alexandria's leg looks weird. I can't."

"Fine," I say.

There's always so much drama with this girl. So she's never seen a dead body. I get that. Has she never seen an injury either? Or maybe she's seen both. Something really bad happened when she was a kid. That's why she's so scared. I should give her a break. But it's so annoying.

We head back to Alexandria. "Are you okay?" I'm getting tired of asking. Someone needs to ask if *I'm* okay.

Chapter 14

Seeking Shelter

Cole can't go anywhere alone. Alexandria can't walk. That leaves me to carry her. It's possible for a little while. But it won't be all the way back to the resort.

This requires extra thought. "Let's wait," I finally say. "Help will be coming soon."

Alexandria makes a face. Cole kicks a snowball.

Waiting is a good plan. But only for the first 20 minutes. Then the wind starts to pick up. Dark clouds fill the sky.

A snowflake lands on my goggles. Then hundreds are falling. Pretty soon, I'm shivering. Please, no. Don't let me get buried again. "We've got to do something," I say.

"We could build an igloo," Alexandria says.

It's not a bad idea. Though I think she means a snow

cave. My coach used to tell us stories. They were about his skiing adventures. In one story, there was a blizzard. He made a snow cave. It kept him alive till help came.

"I'm going to look around," I say.

What I'm looking for is not clear. Maybe a snowbank. That might work. I could build a small cave. Off to one side is a big drift of snow. It's worth checking out. But the snow is too soft. It doesn't pack down. This won't work. Besides, it would take too long to build a cave. The storm could pick up anytime.

A few trees are nearby. This gives me an idea. Evergreens have large bottom branches. There could be pockets of space underneath. We can dig in and make a shelter. It's the best option with such little time. But we need to do it now.

When I get back, Cole and Alexandria are asleep. This is not good. "Hey, guys."

Cole jumps. "What? Where am I?"

"It's okay. It's just me."

It takes Alexandria a little longer to wake up. At first I wonder if she's alive. Before I can go over and shake her, her eyes open.

"Here's the plan," I tell them. "See the trees down there?" They look where I'm pointing and nod. "That's where we're going. You'll have to move, Alexandria. Cole will help you onto my back."

Alexandria bites her lip and nods. Cole and I lift her to her good foot. Then Cole helps her onto my back. With her arms around my neck, I stand up. It's surprising how light she feels. Or it's possible that I'm that strong. It was all those drills in ski practice. We'd walk uphill with a partner on our back. At the time, it felt like torture. My legs hurt for days. But it prepared me for this.

The wind is stronger now, so it's hard to stay steady. Cole puts her hand on Alexandria's back. This keeps me balanced. Slowly we get to the trees.

"Okay, Alexandria. I'm going to set you down. You can lean against this tree." Cole and I get her to the ground. "Now we're going to dig a pit." I'm looking at Cole as I say this. She nods. So far, she's been able to focus. Let's hope it lasts.

Chapter 15

Snowboard Marks the Spot

Tree pits are actually a hazard. Skiers don't know they're there. They can fall in headfirst, and then they're trapped. Our pit will be different. It's going to save us. It has to.

"We're going to burrow," I tell Cole. "But we have to work slowly. Or else the snow will fall in on us."

I ease myself down through the snow. When my feet hit the bottom, I'm able to stand. Space will be tight for three. But we'll be safe.

"Okay, Cole," I call up.

She slides down into the pit. There is room for the two of us.

"Clear more space," I tell her. "And start packing the walls. I'll be right back."

When I climb out, Alexandria looks hopeful.

"Is it ready?" she asks through chattering teeth.

The poor girl is freezing. “Almost. You’ll be able to warm up soon.” I’m not 100 percent sure this is true. There’s no telling until we’re down there. But a little hope can go a long way. “Let me get some branches, and we’ll get you moved.”

The branches I grab are for the floor of the pit. “Here, Cole,” I call as I drop them down to her. “Cover the floor with these.”

“Got them!”

“Okay, Alexandria. Here we go.” We slowly move to the edge of the pit. Her legs are over the side. “I’m going in now. Cole and I will be there to help you down. Okay?”

She nods.

“Okay,” I call once inside.

I’ve got hold of her good leg. Cole has her around the waist. Together, we get Alexandria into the pit. She’s gasping for breath.

“Are you okay?” I ask.

Before she can answer, I’m on the way out.

“You’re leaving?” Cole yells.

“Only for a second. Don’t worry.”

We need markers for when they find us. A piece of our gear would work. The wind is blowing snow all around. Soon it’ll be a whiteout. *Where is our stuff? There!* It’s Cole’s snowboard.

Back at the pit, it makes the perfect marker. Someone is sure to see it sticking out of the snow. Before going down, I grab some branches. These will be our roof.

Inside there's no wind. The branches above us keep the snow out. It's not exactly warm. But it's not freezing either. There's just enough room to walk around. This helps us warm up. We're going to make it.

"Is everyone okay?" I ask.

Alexandria nods.

"Sure," says Cole.

Now we wait for what is coming next.

Chapter 16

With Friends like These

Waiting is boring. Ten minutes feels like an hour. Alexandria spends the time staring at her leg. Cole looks at anything but the leg. I feel like I will go insane.

"Let's do something," I say. "Talk or play a game."

Cole wrinkles her nose. "A game? That's for babies."

Oh, shut up! I'm about to lose it. What she thinks is not important right now. It's her fault we're in this mess. If a game will make me feel better? Then we'll play a game.

"Let's just talk," Alexandria says. "A game is too much work."

Her face is so pale.

"Okay," I say. "Let's talk. Cole, you start."

Cole frowns. She's been taking orders from me for a

while. It must be getting to her. But then she starts talking. It's all about Mr. Lee. What is this obsession? Just let it go. Alexandria must be reading my mind. She changes the subject.

"Why did you move here, Dray?"

The question catches me off guard. "Oh. Well, my mom got a new job." They don't need to know the part about Dad leaving.

"Do you miss Montana?"

"Yeah."

Whose bright idea was it to talk? Staring into space would have been better. It's the thought of home and everything I miss. Especially my best friend. She is the total opposite of Cole.

Jamie cares about other people. And she's positive. That's what she'd tell me to do. Think positive. Not just about the storm. About the move to a new city. It's hard. But she wouldn't waste time feeling bad. She'd be out making new friends. Not just waiting for people to talk to her.

A tear slides down my cheek. I wipe it away before it freezes. Then a light goes off in my head. When I get back, I'm going to try harder. Someone will want to be my friend.

There's a girl in English who seems shy. And there's

the guy from the bus. He has a great smile. I'd like to know more about him.

Cole and Alexandria are okay to hang out with. But friendship shouldn't be this hard.

Chapter 17

Two Questions

Wind whistles through the pit. Bits of snow fall through the branches. We're all shivering. Cole and I start to run in place. Our bodies give off some heat.

The storm sounds powerful. If it's bad enough, the resort might close. That means we could be found sooner.

"Let's play a game," Cole says.

But I thought games were for babies. She must be out of it.

A game of I spy doesn't last long. There isn't much to see. So we try 20 questions. Cole starts.

"Person, place, or thing," I ask.

"Person."

"Is it a man?" I ask.

"Yes."

"Is it Mr. Lee?" Alexandria asks.

Cole looks surprised. "How did you know?"

So much for that game. It's hard to hear over the wind anyway. We agree to wait in silence.

Three hours go by. The wind finally dies down. I lift the branches and look out. A huge snow drift is piled up. All but the tip of Cole's board is buried.

A fresh layer of snow covers the mountain. It looks like it did when we got here. That was before I carved my first tracks. Things can change so fast.

Wait. What's that moving? There are people on the hill! They have to see us. It will be dark soon.

"Hey!" I shout, waving my arms. They don't seem to hear or see me. "Cole! Get up here! Now!"

"Okay. I'm coming."

We both wave and yell for help. Finally they wave back. They're both wearing red jackets. Ski patrol! They have a rescue sled with them. Cole and I watch as they ski down the hill.

"They've found us," I call to Alexandria. "We're getting rescued!"

"My leg really hurts," she says.

"Just a few more minutes. Can you hold on?"

"Uh-huh."

A patroller calls out our names.

"Yes! That's us!" I say. "Alexandria is down here in this pit. Her leg is broken."

"How about you two? Are you hurt?"

"No," I say. "Oh! But we did see a body."

"Whoa. Okay," he says. "Do you think you can show us where?"

"Sure."

Now he's talking into his radio. Something about stretchers and a body and backup. His partner waits until he's done. Then they go to help Alexandria. Soon they lift her out and put her on the sled.

Within minutes, engines are revving. Three snowmobiles arrive. One of them is towing a sled.

The patrollers are speaking to one of the drivers. He comes over and asks me about the body. I describe where I think he is. We also talk a little about what happened. He wants to know how we managed to stay safe.

The patrollers leave with Alexandria.

Cole is on one of the snowmobiles.

"I am *not* helping find that body," she says.

Nobody asked you too, I think.

The other driver tells me to get on. I'm not in charge anymore. That is fine with me.

Chapter 18

Help!

The snowmobile powers over rough snow and debris. We pass the chairlift where this all started. It's scary to think how far we got. I never could have made it back alone.

It hits me how lucky we all are. How many people survive an avalanche and a blizzard? It makes me sad for the man who died. That could have been me. Now I'm wondering about him. How sad his family will be.

The driver stops at a first-aid station. Mr. Lee is waiting. It's hard to read his face. Is it a look of worry or anger? Nobody has lectured me so far. Maybe that comes later. After they know you're okay.

Inside I see Cole. Alexandria is there too. She's lying on her back. Her leg is strapped to a splint.

"It's broken," she says.

A nurse examines me. She asks if I'm okay. Finally someone cares.

The good news is that we're all alive. There's no need for me to worry anymore.

Just as I'm feeling warm and sleepy, Mr. Lee comes in. "I'm glad you're all safe," he says.

Is this when he lectures us?

"For now, we're all going home," he says. "We'll talk about consequences later."

Ah, I think.

"Your parents have been called," he adds. "They're here to pick you up."

Mom is quiet on the ride home. Is she going to lecture me? Will I be grounded? I'd feel better if she yelled. Or said anything. This doesn't feel normal.

When we get home, she wants me to rest. "No TV and no computer."

"Just one quick email to Coach. To thank him for what he taught me."

"That's fine," she says.

On my way up the stairs, she stops me.

"Oh, and, Andrea?"

At last. Here it comes. "Yes, Mom?"

"You had me very worried. I'd be angry if I weren't so relieved. I'm also proud of you. The way you took charge. You saved those girls' lives."

Wow! Was not expecting that. "Thanks, Mom."

After the email to Coach, I start to text Jamie. She won't believe what happened. Pretty soon, my eyes start to close. All I want is to get under the covers and sleep. This is the first time I've felt at home here.

The next day, I wake up sore. Every part of me hurts. It takes a lot to stay alive. Thank goodness it's only Sunday. I'm not ready for the drama at school.

Chapter 19

Good News, Bad News

It's the beginning of the week. I'm feeling much better. That doesn't mean I'm in the mood for school.

Today I'm not thinking about fitting in. Who cares what anyone thinks? That includes Cole. She'll hate this sweater I'm wearing. Too bad.

At school, she's waiting for me. Alexandria won't be coming. Her mom told Cole that she's still in a lot of pain. I don't say much on the way to PE.

Mr. Lee is waiting when we get there. A sub is leading the class. He tells us we have a meeting. This is not going to be fun.

We follow him to the office. He and the principal speak to Cole first. After a few minutes, she comes out. Then it's my turn.

"I hear you saved the day," the principal says.

What? No lecture?

"I helped," I say. "But the ski patrol saved us."

"Cole told us about going out-of-bounds."

"I can explain."

"She said it was her idea," he says.

This is a surprise. It would be like her to blame me. Maybe I'm not in that much trouble.

The principal goes on. "I've also spoken to Alexandria. She said you saved her life. You deserve a lot of credit." He and Mr. Lee look at each other. "However," he says. "It never should have happened. As we told Cole. Students are expected to follow rules. It's the same for off-campus activities. What you did violated the rules. Even if it wasn't your idea. You put the school in an impossible position. What if you had been injured? Or worse?"

That was the lecture. Here comes the punishment.

"No field trips for the rest of the year."

"But there is some good news," Mr. Lee says. He hands me a brochure. "I grabbed this for you."

Bright red words are on the cover. "Join the Ski Patrol!"

"I spoke with the head of the team. You impressed them, Andrea. They're always looking for new members. Especially good skiers. And people who want to help others. You showed that out there. I put in a good word for you."

"Really? Do you think I can do it?"

"Absolutely," Mr. Lee says. "But I told them you're going to be busy. You know, with the wrestling team."

My mouth falls open. Seriously? He said there would be consequences. But this is the worst. I'd rather have detention all year.

Mr. Lee has a big smile on his face. "I'm joking about the wrestling," he says. "But not about ski patrol."

I just stare at him. This is the best news.

Monday is not what I expected. First there was good news. I'm going to join the ski patrol. Now all these kids are coming up to me. They want to know about the avalanche.

At lunch, two kids ask to sit with me. One is the shy girl from English. In science, we have to choose lab partners. The guy from the ski bus is in my class. He wants to team up.

Chapter 20

Change of Course

I don't see Cole again until the end of the day. She's waiting at the bus stop. That's odd. Usually she's in detention. When I say hi, she just looks down. I've never seen her look sad. Only bored or mad.

"I hope you're not in too much trouble," she says.

There's a blank look on her face. She's waiting for me to say something. What does she want? An apology? Maybe I'm supposed to ask how she's doing.

"Not at all. It worked out great."

"Oh, good." There are a few seconds of silence. "Well, my bus is here," she says.

What did I think she would say? That she was sorry? That's not who Cole is. It's kind of sad. We'll still talk. But I'm definitely going to make other friends.

Mom isn't waiting for me at home. It's the one day I

want her to be there. Today was the first day of her new job. This gives me an idea. I drop my backpack on the stairs.

Instead of going to my room, I return to the kitchen. I'll surprise her by making dinner. It will be a way to apologize. I haven't been very nice lately.

Dinner is ready when Mom gets home. Spaghetti and salad. She looks tired but surprised.

"This is nice," she says. "You didn't have to. You're probably still worn out."

"I wanted to. To celebrate your first day. How was it?"

Her smile fades. I can see the look in her eyes. She's the one who's worn out.

"Sit down," I say.

She drops into a chair. "This looks good." She takes a bite and smiles. "Mmm."

"I'm sorry, Mom, for being such a brat. There's a lot I haven't told you. About school and the girls from the ski trip."

"Oh, really? What's been going on?"

I tell her about the first few days of school. About Cole and Alexandria. How I tried so hard to fit in with them.

"It must have been stressful," Mom says. "I'm sorry you had to go through that. I feel bad that we had to move."

"Don't. You did what you had to do."

She gives me a little smile. "Yeah."

Now I'm wondering. What has *she* been through? Mom doesn't talk about her problems. We never talk about my dad. And I don't ask.

"On an unrelated subject," she says. "There's something I meant to share with you. The mom of the man who died emailed me. It's a thank-you for what you did. The patrollers might never have found him without you."

"It was awful, Mom."

"Yes," she says. Her tone has suddenly turned serious. "It could have been you."

"I know. You're right. But there is some good news. It's about ski patrol. I'll show you. Let me grab my backpack."

I come back holding the brochure. She takes it from me.

"We need you!" she reads.

"Can I join? Then I can really help save lives."

"Oh, Andrea. That's perfect for you!"

"Right? I can't wait. Thanks, Mom."

"Tell me more about the ski trip," she says.

"Do you mind if we don't talk about it? A lot of negative stuff happened."

"That's fine, honey. I completely understand."

"From now on, it's all about being positive. It's a

promise I made to myself after the avalanche. This will be hard to believe. But going online doesn't even interest me right now. If my friends want to reach me, they know how."

"It sounds like you learned a lot about yourself. Maybe the trip was meant to be."

"Maybe. One thing's for sure. Jamie would be proud of me. I'll start making some new friends. And speaking of new. Will you help me with something? I want to redecorate my room."

WANT TO KEEP READING?

9781680214819

Turn the page for a sneak peek at another book in the Monarch Jungle® series.

Chapter 1

It Wasn't Me

Marta Lopez sat with her head down. Her long dark hair fell around her face. If nobody could see her, she wasn't there. She gazed at a loose thread on her sleeve. Suddenly she felt a nudge.

"Huh?" She looked up.

"Are you listening?" her mom asked. "Mr. Dalton is talking to you."

Mr. Dalton was the principal of Stone Brook High School. "I have witnesses," he said. "They saw you do it."

He put his phone in front of Marta and her mom. "And I have more proof."

Someone had taken a picture of a drawing. It was a donkey with words scribbled under it.

Marta shook her head. Seriously? She loved to draw.

But not on bathroom walls. That was kid stuff. Not something a 15-year-old would do.

And she would never call Mr. King an ass. He was the art teacher. Art was the only class she liked. Besides that, the drawing was bad. If she *had* done this drawing? It would have been good.

"I promise you," Mrs. Lopez said. "My daughter would never do that. She knows better." She moved Marta's hair from her face.

"Stop, Mom." Marta pulled away.

"Tell me you didn't do this," Mr. Dalton said.

Marta knew the truth. But she wasn't talking.

"I'm sorry, Mrs. Lopez. It's important that your daughter learns a lesson." He looked at Marta. "I'm suspending you for three days. I've told your teachers. They will email you any homework. And this will go on your record. Do you understand?"

"Yes," she mumbled.

"And, Marta," he said. "There are only a few weeks until summer break. I urge you to make the rest of the year count. Do your best. And try to stay out of trouble."

The meeting with Mr. Dalton was over. But the drama was just beginning. On the drive home, her mom did most of the talking.

"I swear on all that is holy. I don't know what to do with you. Or what to say."

"Then don't say anything," Marta said softly.

"Shut your mouth!" her mom shot back. "Don't you dare say another word. I missed work for this. That's half a day's pay. And for what? To hear good things? No. To hear that you're a vandal."

Here we go, Marta thought. There was nothing she could do. Her mom was not going to stop.

"Your dad and I have tried to be patient. But we're tired of your moods. The way you mope around. You don't even talk to us. All you do is sit in your room and draw. Draw, draw, draw. In that little notepad. Thank God for the A in art. At least you have one good grade."

Marta stared out the window.

"There's no excuse. You're a smart girl. And so pretty. Why do you hide it? Just look at your clothes. That big shirt and baggy pants. And your hair. You never comb it. No wonder you have no friends."

That last comment wasn't fair. It was true that Marta didn't have friends. But it wasn't her fault.

For most of her life, her parents had been farmworkers. That meant they had to move a lot. Her dad had a phrase for it. *Following the harvest*. They picked onions in Texas. Lettuce in California. Berries in Michigan.

With each move, it was like starting over. She was the new girl all over again. It was hard to make friends.

It took time, but her parents got better jobs. Now they worked at a factory that canned fruit.

Both worked the canning line. They washed and peeled fruit and filled containers. Her dad made sure the line was set up properly. He also cleaned the equipment.

The factory canned other foods too. The work was year-round. So far, they'd had the same day shift. But that could always change. It depended on when crops came in. Sometimes one or both of them worked overtime.

Even with extra hours, it didn't add up to much money. But the family could stay in one place. It was a better life for their daughters. "More normal," they had said.

Marta struggled with the idea of "normal." What did that even mean? For her it was still a lonely life. She wasn't able to make friends. But she didn't try either.

Her mom's voice broke through her thoughts.

"Your grades have to get better. Do you hear me?" she said. "It's your only chance for a good life. Don't you get that? Or do you want to work in the fields? I know I don't want that life again."

No, Marta didn't want that life. But she couldn't picture what her life would be.